Harp Seal Pups

BY **Downs Matthews**

PHOTOGRAPHS BY **Dan Guravich**

SIMON & SCHUSTER BOOKS FOR YOUNG READERS

Also by Downs Matthews
and Dan Guravich

Arctic Foxes
Wetlands
Arctic Summer
Polar Bear Cubs
Skimmers

SIMON & SCHUSTER BOOKS FOR YOUNG READERS
An imprint of Simon & Schuster Children's Publishing Division
1230 Avenue of the Americas
New York, New York 10020
Text copyright © 1997 by Downs Matthews
Photographs copyright © 1997 by Dan Guravich
All rights reserved including the right of reproduction in whole or in part in any form.
SIMON & SCHUSTER BOOKS FOR YOUNG READERS is a trademark of Simon & Schuster.
Book design by Diane DePasque
The text of this book is set in Versailles Light
Manufactured in Singapore
First Edition
10 9 8 7 6 5 4 3 2 1
Library of Congress Cataloging-in-Publication Data
Matthews, Downs.
Harp seal pups / by Downs Matthews ; photographs by Dan Guravich.
p.   cm.
1. Harp seal—Juvenile literature.   2. Harp seal—Infancy—Juvenile literature.
3. Harp seal—Saint Lawrence, Gulf of—Juvenile literature.
[1. Harp seal.   2. Seals (Animals)]   I. Guravich, Dan, ill.   II. Title.
QL737.P64M36   1997   599.74'8—dc20   95-2314   CIP   AC
ISBN: 0-689-80014-2

In memory of author Richard Davids,
whose early interest in the Far North
helped direct public attention to the unique
qualities of Arctic wildlife.

The poet Homer called seals "brine children" that live in the "fish-cold" sea. And so they do. Millions of seals live in the brine, or salty seawater, of the North Atlantic, for example. Here it is so cold that the ocean freezes in winter. There are fish to eat and clean waters to swim in. This is the perfect environment for a certain kind of seal known as the harp seal.

Although harp seals are used to the cold, icy waters, they are actually warm-blooded mammals like dogs and cats or monkeys or human beings. They are like large dogs that have learned to live in the sea.

Harp seals have coats of silvery gray fur. They are called harp seals because the black pattern on their backs and sides resembles a harp. Adult male harp seals weigh up to three hundred pounds. Adult females are less heavy. They are both about as long as a human is tall.

Harp seals are often referred to as Greenland seals because they were first seen on the island of Greenland. All summer long, over three million harp seals swim and fish around this island and off the Arctic coast of Canada. In November, when the northern seas begin to freeze, harp seals go south so that mother seals can give birth to their pups.

Mother seals look for a place where the temperature is not so cold and where polar bears can't find them. There are four such places: in the White Sea, off the coast of Russia; in the Greenland Sea, near Jan Mayen Island; in the North Atlantic Ocean, off the coast of Labrador; and in the Gulf of Saint Lawrence, near the coast of Canada. There the harp seal mothers know their pups will be safe.

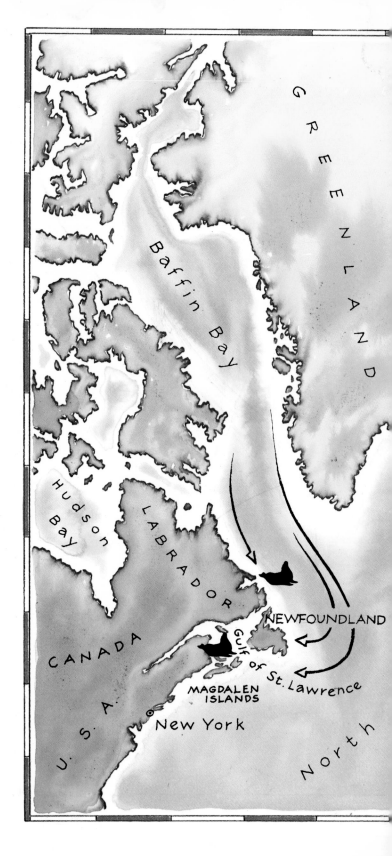

During winter almost a million harp seals rest on the ice that covers the Gulf of Saint Lawrence. Stormy winds and currents break the ice into big slabs called floes. Open water lies between the floes. These openings are called leads. Seals surface in the leads and crawl out of the water onto the ice.

A harp seal uses its large paddlelike hind flippers to swim. The flipper spreads open and then closes, like the fingers of a hand. The seal swims by bringing a closed flipper forward and opening it. Then it pushes backward with the flipper to thrust itself forward through the water. When a harp seal swims, it seems to wave its hind flippers back and forth. Its front flippers are small and bony, with long sharp nails. The seal uses its claws to crawl on the slippery ice.

When swimming, harp seals close their noses tightly to shut out water. When a harp seal breathes, it must open its nose. It can hold its breath for a long time. A harp seal can stay underwater for as long as fifteen minutes, and it can dive down more than eight hundred feet in search of food.

Because harp seal eyes are large, they can see well underwater, where the light is dim. Tears flow over the eyes and wash them free of salt and sand.

When they wish to rest or sleep, harp seals crawl out of the water and onto the ice. A nap for a harp seal lasts only a minute or two. The seal must look out for hunters, both animal and human, that might want to kill it for food.

In the water, a harp seal must avoid killer whales, walruses, and Greenland sharks. If no harm comes to it, a harp seal may live as long as thirty years.

In February the harp seals swim under the ice to a part of the Gulf of Saint Lawrence near the Magdalen Islands. There each mother seal prepares for the birth in March of her one pup. She finds a lead and crawls out onto the ice. She uses the same lead so often that when the water in the lead freezes, a hole stays open where the seal comes and goes. This is called an entry hole.

With a thrust of her flippers, a female harp seal leaps out of her entry hole and onto the snowy surface. Around her are thousands and thousands of other females. They form a huge nursery for their babies. Male seals mostly keep to themselves. They go to the edge of the ice floes and sleep.

In March, when she is ready to give birth, the female seal chooses a place on the ice near her entry hole. Other females may come near, but she warns them away. She arches her body and lifts her chin and growls. If an intruder doesn't heed her threats, the mother-to-be will strike at the other seal with her claws and try to bite her.

Birth takes less than a minute. When her baby appears, the mother spins around and touches her nose to her pup's. She smells its breath and its body. In that instant she learns her baby's special odor. She will use that odor to locate her own pup among all the other seal pups in the huge nursery. She studies her pup and listens to its cries. She will nurse no baby but her own.

This new pup is a girl. She is about two feet long and weighs about fifteen pounds. For two days her fur will have a yellow color, and then it will turn pure white. The pup has a black nose and eyes and black marks on her face that look like eyebrows. At this age, harp seal pups are called whitecoats.

The baby's fur protects her from the cold. But she is thin. She needs fat to stay warm. She drinks her mother's rich milk and grows a layer of fat called blubber. The mother seal lies on her side. She calls to her daughter. The pup squirms over the ice by pushing with her hind feet. The mother has two nipples, and her daughter sucks first one and then the other. The mother feeds her pup every three hours, night and day.

After a meal the mother and daughter sleep on the ice. The pup always sleeps in the same place. The heat of her body melts the ice to form a little ice cradle. When she wakes up, she begins to cry for food. Her calls sound like *"Maa, maa."*

Right away, the pup begins to grow. She gets plump with blubber and grows longer and longer. Each day she gains five pounds.

The whitecoat's mother dives down her entry hole to swim under the ice in search of fish. She needs to eat about eight pounds of fish every day. She feeds mainly on fish that human beings don't eat. Every few minutes she comes back to see if her baby is safe.

While her mother is away, the pup sees another female seal. She crawls over to her, thinking she might be her mother. But the strange female pushes the pup away. The pup doesn't understand. She wanders over the ice and calls for her mother. Soon she is far from home.

In the meantime, her mother returns from fishing. She leaps onto the ice and looks for her baby. But the little whitecoat is not where she is supposed to be. The mother crawls over to the spot where she left her daughter and sniffs. She smells the odor of her pup on the ice.

Then she begins to croon a high-pitched trill. It sounds a little like a softly blown police whistle.

The mother approaches other babies nearby. Their mothers rush over to drive away the intruder. She moves farther and farther from her entry hole. She calls and calls.

Then from far away she hears a little whimpering cry. *"Maa! Maa!"* The mother recognizes the sound of her daughter. She begins to crawl quickly toward the baby. The pup squirms over the snow to her mother. The mother smells her daughter and knows that the pup is hers.

Now she wants her pup to go back to their home by the entry hole. First she lies down on her side. The pup comes to her to suckle. Her mother crawls away a few yards, moving toward the entry hole. Again she offers the pup a meal, and the pup goes to her. Once more she crawls away, calling to the pup to follow. When she has lured her baby back to her own space by the entry hole, the mother lies down and lets her daughter feed.

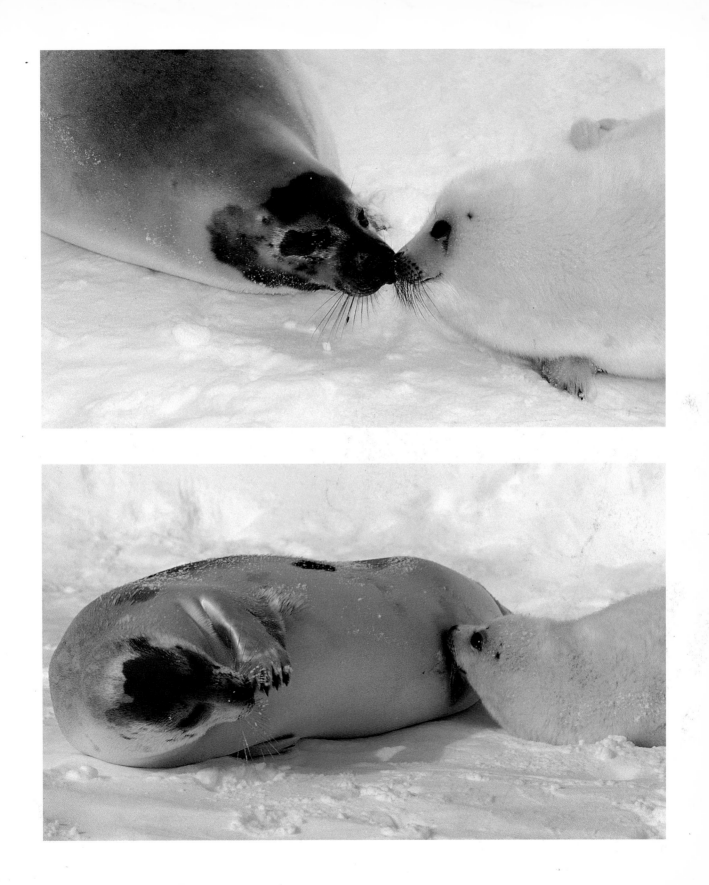

After twelve days the pup grows so large that she weighs about eighty pounds. She is so fat with blubber that she looks like a big white pillow. She stores the blubber as food.

Now the pup is becoming a teenager. Her gray adult coat begins to show through her white baby hair. We call these young seals graycoats.

At this age, the mother stops feeding her pup and leaves her to fend for herself. At first, the young graycoat calls and cries, but no one comes. For several days, she sleeps on the ice all alone. She doesn't need to eat right away: her blubber keeps her well fed.

Ragged jacket

Beater

Bedlamer

When she is twenty-one days old, the graycoat starts to grow a new fur coat. All her white hair falls out and a coat of short gray hair grows in its place. While this is happening, her coat looks ragged and torn. We call these pups ragged jackets.

When she is twenty-five days old and her adult coat has grown in, the young ragged jacket must learn to swim. When she practices swimming, she looks as if she is beating the water with her flippers. This is why we call seals of this age beaters.

The young beater grows stronger and larger. She learns to swim swiftly and to twist and turn in the water. Her swimming skills help her to catch little fish and shrimplike animals to eat. Now she can live on her own.

Once she is a year old, the young seal will be called a bedlamer. The name comes from French words that mean "beast of the sea."

In May, the bedlamer is nearly as large as her mother. As the ice melts, she swims north with the others. The harp seal herd returns to the waters of the North Atlantic. All summer they fish and sleep and grow fat while waiting for winter to come again.